For Charlie
—J.M.

For Johann
—M.S.

E
MAR

Good Thing You're Not an Octopus!
Text copyright © 2001 by Julie Markes
Illustrations copyright © 2001 by Maggie Smith
Printed in the U.S.A. All rights reserved.
www.harperchildrens.com

Library of Congress Cataloging-in-Publication Data
Markes, Julie.
Good thing you're not an octopus! / by Julie Markes ;
pictures by Maggie Smith.   p.   cm.
Summary: A little boy finds that his life is pretty easy compared to how it might be.
ISBN 0-06-028465-X. — ISBN 0-06-028466-8 (lib. bdg.)
[1. Animals—Fiction.   2. Self-acceptance—Fiction.]
I. Smith, Maggie, 1965–   ill.   II. Title.
III. Title: Good thing you are not an octopus.
PZ7.M339454Go   2001   99-37139   [E]—dc21

Typography by Elynn Cohen
1 2 3 4 5 6 7 8 9 10 ❖ First Edition

Good Thing You're Not an
OCTOPUS!

Story by **Julie Markes** • Pictures by **Maggie Smith**

HarperCollins Publishers

You don't like to
get dressed in the morning?

It's a good thing

you're not an octopus.

If you were an octopus,
you would have *eight* legs
to put in your pants!

You don't like to put on your shoes?

It's a good thing

you're not a caterpillar.

If you were a caterpillar,
you would have *sixteen* feet
to put shoes on!

You don't like to
ride in your car seat?

It's a good thing

you're not a kangaroo.

If you were a baby kangaroo,
you'd have to ride
in your mother's pouch!

You don't like to eat your lunch?

It's a good thing

you're not a bird.

If you were a bird,
you would have to eat
worms for lunch!

You don't like
to take a nap?

It's a good thing

you're not a bear.

If you were a bear,
you would have to nap
all winter long!

You don't like
to take a bath?

It's a good thing

you're not a tiger.

If you were a baby tiger,
your mother would have
to lick you clean!

You don't like to
brush your teeth?

It's a good thing

you're not a shark.

If you were a shark,
you could have *two hundred*
teeth to brush!

So, the next time you need to

get dressed,

go for a ride,

eat your lunch,

take a nap,

take a bath,

or brush your teeth,

remember:

It's a good thing you're YOU!

PHEW!